First published in *Fairy Tales* 2000 by Walker Books Ltd
87 Vauxhall Walk, London SE11 5HJ

This edition published 2003

2 4 6 8 10 9 7 5 3 1

Text © 2000 Berlie Doherty
Illustrations © 2000 Jane Ray

The right of Berlie Doherty and Jane Ray to be identified respectively
as the author and illustrator of this work has been asserted by them
in accordance with the Copyright, Designs and Patents Act 1988

This book has been typeset in Palatino

Printed in China

British Library Cataloguing in Publication Data:
a catalogue record for this book is available from the British Library

ISBN 0-7445-9879-6

www.walkerbooks.co.uk

Hansel
and
Gretel

BERLIE DOHERTY
illustrated by JANE RAY

WALKER BOOKS
AND SUBSIDIARIES
LONDON • BOSTON • SYDNEY

It was a long time ago and a long way away. A boy called Hansel and a girl called Gretel lived with their parents in a cottage by the forest. Times were hard – wolves stole the sheep, foxes stole the hen, the potatoes didn't grow. They were nearly starving, and one night when the children were so hungry that they couldn't sleep, they heard their mother saying, "Husband,

husband, there's not enough food left for all of us."

"But what can we do?" they heard their father say.

"Husband, husband, it's quite simple. We must take the children into the forest and leave them to fend for themselves."

"I can't do that," he said.

"If we don't, husband, then we'll all die."

Gretel began to cry then, and Hansel put his arms round her. "Don't worry," he said. "I know what to do."

He waited till his parents were asleep and then he crept outside. The moon was full and bright, and the pebbles on the ground shone like stars. He filled his pockets with them.

Next morning they were woken up by their mother shaking them roughly. "Get up, get up. You must come with us to chop wood." She gave them each a slice of bread, but Hansel slipped his into Gretel's pocket, and they all set off together. Every now and again Hansel lingered behind to drop a pebble on the path.

"Come on, come on," his father urged, anxious to get it all over and done with.

"What are you gawping at, stupid boy?" his mother asked.

"I'm just saying goodbye to my little white cat," Hansel said as he dropped another pebble.

"That's not a cat, you fool. How many times must I tell you! It's the sun shining on the chimney pot!"

When they arrived in the middle of the forest the parents told the children to gather twigs and light a fire. "And wait here till we come for you." They went off without saying goodbye.

The children ate their bread and curled up by the fire. They could hear a sound like the chop, chop, chop of an axe and thought for a long time that it must be their father near by, but it was only a branch knocking against a pole that their mother had set up to trick them. It grew dark and cold, their little fire died out. But when the moon came up, there were the pebbles that Hansel

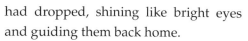

had dropped, shining like bright eyes and guiding them back home.

When they knocked on the door and their mother opened it she couldn't believe what she was seeing. "Husband! Husband! The children have come home!" She scolded them for staying out so long, but their father's heart rose at the sight of his children.

"We will make do on what we have," he told his wife, and she pursed her lips grimly and said, "We'll have to see, husband."

But bad times came again. The earth was cold and bare, men and beasts groaned with hunger. One night the children lay awake and heard their mother saying, "Husband, husband, something's got to be done. Tomorrow we'll take the children to the forest and leave them there."

Gretel cried, and Hansel put his arms round her and said, "Don't worry, Gretel. I'll think of something." When his parents were asleep he crept downstairs. Outside, the white pebbles gleamed in the moonlight, but his mother had locked the door and he couldn't get to them.

Next morning they had to get up early. "Come on, come on," the children's mother called. "We've got to get some wood for our fire." She gave them a much smaller slice of bread than last time. "Keep it in your pocket for later," she told them.

But every now and again as they walked Hansel lingered behind and crumbled little pieces of bread on to the ground to guide the way back home.

"What are you hanging back there for?" his mother called.

"I'm only looking at the little white dove on our rooftop. It's saying goodbye to me."

"Stupid boy, there's no white dove," his mother snapped. "It's our chimney pot, I keep telling you!"

They walked and walked until there was no walking left in their feet. "Have a rest," their mother told them. "Light a fire and sit here until we come back." And she and her husband went off without saying goodbye.

Hansel had crumbled all his slice of bread away, so they only had Gretel's piece to share between them. Night was falling; it was growing dark, and their little fire went down. The moon came up and the children searched for the trail of breadcrumbs that would lead them back home, but there was nothing left. The birds of the forest had eaten every crumb.

Hansel and Gretel built up their fire again and covered themselves over with leaves, and tried to shut out the howling and creaking night. When morning came they set off for home again, but the more they walked, the more they got lost, and sometimes it seemed that they passed the same tree eleven times in an hour.

They wandered for three nights and three days, and nothing looked right. Nothing looked like the way home, and the trees were high and dark, blocking out the light of day.

"Follow me! Follow me!" they heard a voice calling, and they saw a white bird gleaming like the moon among the branches. They ran after it, and came to a clearing, and there in the middle was a cottage made of gingerbread.

They went right up to it, quite sure that they must be dreaming, but it was true. Hansel pulled a piece of brandy-snap off the gate and gave Gretel some. Gretel picked two lollipops out of the garden and handed one to Hansel. "Mmm! Taste the door – it's like

strawberries!" Hansel said. But Gretel was too busy licking the barley sugar windows. They couldn't stop themselves. They pulled great chunks of sweet and sticky gingerbread out of the wall and stuffed them into their mouths. The more they ate, the more they wanted.

They heard a voice coming from inside, "Who's that nibbling at my house?"

"It's only a little harvest mouse!" they called, and carried on eating. But then the door opened, and out came the oldest woman in the world. They stopped with their hands full and their cheeks bulging, and stared. Her skin shivered and crinkled like dry leaves and her eyes were as red as burning coals. She was a witch on the look-out for children to eat. But she seemed sweet enough at first. "Come right in," she cooed, just like the white bird. "I've been expecting you." They followed her inside the house and there sure enough was a table laid for two with still more food, and upstairs, two beds with clean white sheets.

Hansel and Gretel slept like angels on white clouds that night. But next morning Gretel woke up to find the witch patting Hansel's rosy cheeks as if they were ripe apples. "He'll do nicely," she crooned. "When he's fattened up a bit more."

"What do you mean?" said Gretel,

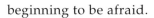

beginning to be afraid.

"You've had your feast – now I want mine," snapped the witch, all her cooey sweetness gone. She yanked Hansel out of bed and pushed him into a cage in the yard before he had time to blink the sleep out of his eyes. "Now get him fed," she yapped at Gretel. "I like nice fat boys for my supper."

From then on all the best food went to Hansel. Gretel got bread crusts and bits of bacon rind and stale cakes. But she didn't mind about that, she was just worried about poor Hansel. He wasn't enjoying his food much either. Every day the witch told him to put his finger out of the cage so she could squeeze it and see how much fatter he was getting.

He played a trick on her. He stuck a bit
of chicken bone out of the cage instead
of his finger, and the witch's eyesight

was so bad that she couldn't tell the difference. But she decided at last that she was too hungry to wait any longer.

"Today's the day!" she said, smacking her lips. "Get a fire going, Gretel. I've a tasty stew to cook."

She filled a cauldron with water and started chopping up vegetables, and as she was chopping she cackled a happy song to herself:

"Carrots and onions in the pot,
  And a fat little boy
      when it's good and hot."

She threw in the vegetables one by one.

Gretel began to cry.

"Gretel," the witch called. "I'm going to make some bread to mop up the gravy. Get the bread tray out of the oven for me."

"Nothing tastes better than
little boy stew
With slices of little girl bread to chew,"

she sang in her crackly voice. "Hurry up, Gretel. The bread tray."

Gretel knew what the witch was going to do. She wasn't going to bake bread at all, she was going to bake *her*. She went to the oven with her heart in her boots.

"I can't turn the handle. It's too stiff," she cried.

"What a useless child you are. Bang it with the poker. Like this." And the witch did it for her.

"But I can't see the bread tray. It's too dark in the oven," Gretel cried.

"What a stupid girl you are. Bend down and reach right in. Like this."

And the witch bent down to do it for her, and quick as a flash Gretel shoved her into the oven and slammed the door. And that was the end of the witch. Burnt to a cinder.

Then Gretel ran to Hansel's cage and let him out. They loaded up their pockets with all the pearls and diamonds that the witch had in her cupboards, and ran and ran from the gingerbread house, ran and ran from the dark forest and the tall trees, and at last they came to their own cottage with its white chimneys.

There was their father, grown old and ill with worrying about them. His wife was dead and gone. He wept when he saw the children. "I thought I would never see you again," he said.

Hansel and Gretel gave him the treasure they had taken from the witch's house, and they all lived in great happiness, and were never hungry again.

A MESSAGE TO PARENTS

Reading good books to young children is a crucial factor in a child's psychological and intellectual development. It promotes a mutually warm and satisfying relationship between parent and child and enhances the child's awareness of the world around him. It stimulates the child's imagination and lays a foundation for the development of the skills necessary to support the critical thinking process. In addition, the parent who reads to his child helps him to build vocabulary and other prerequisite skills for the child's own successful reading.

In order to provide parents and children with books which will do these things, Brown Watson has published this series of small books specially designed for young children. These books are factual, fanciful, humorous, questioning and adventurous. A library acquired in this inexpensive way will provide many hours of pleasurable and profitable reading for parents and children.

The Cock,
The Mouse
And The
Little Red
Hen

By Helen Adler
Illustrated by Shelley Thornton

Brown Watson

ENGLAND

Once upon a time there was a hill, and on the hill there was a pretty little house. It had a little green door and four little windows with green shutters, and in it there lived a cock, a mouse, and a little red hen.

On another hill close by, there was another little house. It had a door that wouldn't shut, and all the paint was worn off the shutters. In this house there lived a big bad fox and three bad little foxes.

One morning these three bad little foxes said to Big Bad Fox, "Oh, Father, we're so hungry!"

Big Bad Fox shook his head and said, "On the hill over there I see a house. In that house there lives Cock—"

"Mouse and Little Red Hen!" screamed the three bad little foxes.

"They are nice and fat," Big Bad Fox went on. "This very day I'll take my sack and go up that hill to that house, and into my sack I will put Cock and Mouse and Little Red Hen."

Meanwhile, what were Cock and Mouse and Little Red Hen doing?

Well, sad to say, Cock and Mouse had both got out of bed on the wrong side that morning. They came grumbling down to the kitchen where Little Red Hen was bustling about.

"Who'll get breakfast ready?" she asked.

"Not I," said Cock.

"Nor I," said Mouse.

"Then I'll do it myself," said Little Red Hen.

All through breakfast Cock and Mouse grumbled. Cock upset the milk and Mouse scattered crumbs upon the floor.

"Who'll clear away the breakfast?" asked
Little Red Hen.

"Not I," said Cock.

"Nor I," said Mouse.

"Then I'll do it myself," said Little Red Hen,
and she cleared everything away.

"Now, who'll help me make the beds?" asked Little Red Hen.

"Not I," said Cock.

"Nor I," said Mouse.

"Then I'll do it myself," said Little Red Hen, and she tripped away upstairs.

Then grumpy Cock and lazy Mouse sat down by the fire and fell asleep.

Now Big Bad Fox had crept up the hill, and if Cock and Mouse hadn't been asleep, they would have seen him peeping through the window.

Rat-tat-tat! Fox knocked at the door.

"It's the postman, perhaps," said Mouse, half opening his eyes. "He may have a letter for me." So Mouse went to see who it was. He lifted the latch, and as soon as the door was open, in jumped Big Bad Fox.

"Oh! Oh! Oh!" squeaked Mouse as he tried to run up the chimney.

"Doodle doodle do!" screamed Cock as he jumped on the back of the biggest chair.

But Fox only laughed as he took the little
mouse by the tail and dropped him into the
sack. He seized Cock by the neck and popped
him in too.

The poor little red hen came running downstairs to see what all the noise was about, and Fox put her into the sack with the others.

Then Big Bad Fox took a long piece of string from his pocket and wound it around the mouth of the sack. He threw the sack over his back, and set off down the hill.

"Oh, I wish I hadn't been so cross," said Cock.

"Oh! I wish I hadn't been so lazy," said Mouse.

"It's never too late to mend," said Little Red Hen. "Don't be too sad. See, I have my workbag here, and in it is a pair of scissors and a needle and thread. Very soon you will see what I am going to do."

Now the sun was very hot, and soon Big Bad Fox's sack began to feel very heavy. "I will lie down under a tree and rest," he said. So he threw the sack down and very soon was fast asleep. "Snore, snore, snore," went Fox.

When Little Red Hen heard this, she took out her scissors and snipped a hole in the sack just big enough for Mouse to creep through.

"Quick," she whispered to Mouse, "go and get a stone just as large as yourself."

Out ran Mouse, and soon he came back with a stone.

"Push it in here," said Little Red Hen. So he pushed it into the bag.

Then Little Red Hen snipped a hole that was large enough for Cock to get through.

"Quick," she said, "run and get a stone as big as yourself."

Out flew Cock, and soon he came back with a big stone, which he pushed into the sack, too.

Then Little Red Hen popped out, got a stone as big as herself, and pushed it in.

Next she took out her needle and thread, and sewed up the hole.

When she was done, Cock and Mouse and Little Red Hen quickly ran home, shut the door behind them, and soon felt quite safe.

Big Bad Fox slept under the tree for some time, but at last he awoke.

"Dear, dear," he said, rubbing his eyes and then looking at the long shadows on the grass, "how late it is getting. I must hurry home."

So Big Bad Fox went groaning down the hill,
till he came to a stream. Splash! In went one
foot. Splash! In went the other, but the stones
in the sack were so heavy that at the very
next step, down tumbled Big Bad Fox into a
deep pool.

The fishes carried him off to their caves and kept him prisoner there, so he was never seen again. And the three greedy little foxes had to go to bed without any supper.

But Cock and Mouse never grumbled again. They lit the fire, filled the kettle, made the breakfast, and did all the work while good Little Red Hen had a holiday

No foxes ever troubled them again, and they are still living happily in the little house with the little green door and green shutters that stands on the hill.

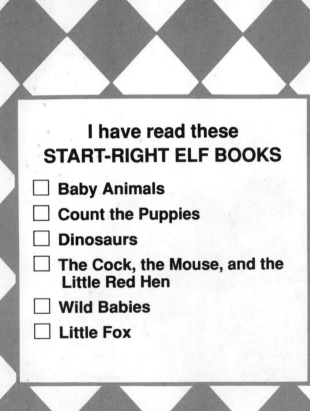

**I have read these
START-RIGHT ELF BOOKS**

☐ **Baby Animals**

☐ **Count the Puppies**

☐ **Dinosaurs**

☐ **The Cock, the Mouse, and the
Little Red Hen**

☐ **Wild Babies**

☐ **Little Fox**